A Note to Parents

Welcome to REAL KIDS READERS, a series of phonics-based books for children who are beginning to read. In the classroom, educators use phonics to teach children how to sound out unfamiliar words, providing a firm foundation for reading skills. At home, you can use REAL KIDS READERS to reinforce and build on that foundation, because the books follow the same basic phonic guidelines that children learn in school.

Of course the best way to help your child become a good reader is to make the experience fun—and REAL KIDS READERS do that, too. With their realistic story lines and lively characters, the books engage children's imaginations. With their clean design and sparkling photographs, they provide picture clues that help new readers decipher the text. The combination is sure to entertain young children and make them truly want to read.

REAL KIDS READERS have been developed at three distinct levels to make it easy for children to read at their own pace.

- LEVEL 1 is for children who are just beginning to read.
- LEVEL 2 is for children who can read with help.
- LEVEL 3 is for children who can read on their own.

A controlled vocabulary provides the framework at each level. Repetition, rhyme, and humor help increase word skills. Because children can understand the words and follow the stories, they quickly develop confidence. They go back to each book again and again, increasing their proficiency and sense of accomplishment, until they're ready to move on to the next level. The result is a rich and rewarding experience that will help them develop a lifelong love of reading.

For Mom
—L. P.

Special thanks to Lands' End, Dodgeville, WI, for providing clothing
and to Converse for providing sneakers.

Produced by DWAI / Seventeenth Street Productions, Inc.
Reading Specialist: Virginia Grant Clammer

Library of Congress Cataloging-in-Publication Data
Papademetriou, Lisa.
  You're in big trouble, Brad / Lisa Papademetriou ; photographs by Dorothy Handelman.
      p.   cm. — (Real kids readers. Level 3)
  Summary: Called to the principal's office, Brad remembers all the tricks he has
played on his classmates and wonders who has turned him in.
  ISBN 0-7613-2022-9 (lib. bdg.) — ISBN 0-7613-2047-4 (pbk.).
  [1. Behavior—Fiction. 2. Schools—Fiction.] I. Handelman, Dorothy, ill.
II. Title. III. Series.
PZ7.P1954Yo   1998
[E]—dc21   98-11026
                                                           CIP
                                                           AC

pbk: 10 9 8 7 6 5 4 3 2 1
lib: 10 9 8 7 6 5 4 3 2 1

You're in Big Trouble, Brad!

By Lisa Papademetriou
Photographs by Dorothy Handelman

M

The Millbrook Press

Brookfield, Connecticut

Brad peeked into his backpack. Inside, he had a big surprise for his teacher, Ms. Carter. He couldn't wait to leave it on her desk.

"*Ribbit!*" said the surprise.

It was a frog.

"Shhh," Brad said to the frog. "Be quiet, or you'll get us in trouble."

Brad loved playing tricks on people, but he hated getting caught. So far, he'd been pretty lucky.

6

"Are you paying attention, Brad?" asked Ms. Carter.

"Yes, Ms. Carter," said Brad. He smiled sweetly at his teacher.

"Then why are you talking to your backpack?" she asked.

The class laughed, and Brad felt a little silly. "Oh, well," he thought. "Soon they'll have something else to laugh at. Something green with webbed feet!"

Just then a woman's voice came over the intercom. "Good morning," said the voice.

The kids all froze. That voice belonged to the principal, Dr. Simms. She was very strict.

"Bradley Farmer," Dr. Simms went on. "Please come to my office right away. Thank you."

Brad wasn't used to being called Bradley. It took him a minute to realize that Dr. Simms meant him!

Eve, the girl who sat in front of Brad, turned around. She gave him a mean smile. "You're in big trouble, Brad," she said.

Brad made a face back, but his heart was pounding. Which trick was he in trouble for? It was hard to guess—there were so many! But one thing was for sure. He did not want to go to the principal's office.

"Well, Brad," said Ms. Carter. "You heard Dr. Simms. It's time to go."

"But, Ms. Carter, I can't!" said Brad.

His teacher frowned. "Why not?"

"Because . . . because . . . it's my turn to feed the fish today," Brad said. He hurried over to the fish tank.

"I think they'll live while you talk to the principal," Ms. Carter said.

"Maybe so," Brad said. "But what if there's a flood in the basement or the roof caves in? I'm the line leader this week. What if you need me to lead the class outside?"

"I guess we'll just have to get along without you," said Ms. Carter.

Very slowly, Brad got ready to go. "I'll need to take my books," he said.

"Brad," said Ms. Carter.

"And my pencil case and my folders and my notebook," said Brad.

"Brad!" said Ms. Carter. "Leave those things here and just go."

Brad sighed. He put everything back.

His teacher smiled at him. "Don't worry. You'll be fine," she said.

Brad grabbed his backpack and headed for the door.

"*Ribbit*," said the backpack.

"What was that?" asked Ms. Carter.

"Um . . . that was a hiccup," said Brad. "Excuse me!"

"Good luck, Brad. You'll need it!" said Eve. And she gave him another mean grin.

A moment later, Brad was alone in the hall. He started walking. Soon he would have to face the principal.

Who could have told on him?

"Maybe it was Eve," he said out loud. His voice sounded creepy in the empty hall. But he smiled, remembering the trick he had pulled on her. . . .

Eve had a fancy lunch box that she always bragged about. Every time she opened it, she would say, "Isn't my lunch box cool? Look, the cup and plate and spoon all match."

Brad didn't like Eve's bragging. He wanted to teach her a lesson.

Eve kept her lunch box next to her desk, right in front of Brad. One day, when Eve was busy reading, he grabbed the lunch box. Then he pulled something out of his backpack.

It was a snake!

The snake was made of rubber, but it looked very real. Brad put it into Eve's lunch box. Then he pushed the lunch box across the floor to Eve's desk.

When Eve opened her lunch box, she let out a scream. It was very loud!

Brad hid his smile and pretended to be just as surprised as she was. Too bad he couldn't ask for his snake back. But at least Eve never bragged about her lunch box again!

Had Eve guessed that he was behind the trick and told on him? Maybe—or maybe not. Matt could have been the one too.

Brad thought about the trick he had pulled on Matt. . . .

Matt used to do everything Brad did. When Brad started wearing a black cap to school, Matt got one and wore it to school too. If Brad brought apple juice for lunch, the next day Matt did too. And if Brad checked out a library book, Matt checked out another one on the same subject.

Brad did not want Matt to copy him. He thought that Matt should just be himself. So Brad came up with a plan.

One day, right before recess, Brad lay down in the hall. He put his ear to the floor.

Matt came over. "What are you doing?" he asked.

"Shhh! Please be quiet," said Brad.

"Why?" Matt asked. "What are you listening to?"

"I'm listening to the floor," said Brad.

"I want to listen too," said Matt. He lay down next to Brad and put his ear to the floor. "What are we listening for?"

"Shhh," Brad said. "We're listening for sounds."

"Okay," Matt said.

The two boys lay still for a while. They did not speak.

29

Finally Brad got up. "I'll be right back," he said. "Keep listening." Then he went outside to play kick ball with his friends.

Matt had gotten in trouble with Ms. Carter for lying on the floor. After that, he stopped copying Brad.

Now Brad walked slowly down the hall. Had Matt figured out that it was all a trick? Had he told Dr. Simms what had happened? Or had someone else told on him?

Brad remembered the time he'd tricked the whole class. . . .

There were two doors to Ms. Carter's classroom. Once, while everyone was at lunch, Brad made two signs that said "Please use other door." Then he taped a sign to each door.

When his classmates came back to the room, they got all confused. They ended up waiting in the hall until Ms. Carter returned and took down the signs.

Brad chewed on a fingernail. There were other reasons why he might be in trouble. Once he made chalk-dust fog in the classroom. Another time, at lunch, he squirted milk through his nose on purpose.

Brad was very nervous. What would Dr. Simms do to punish him? Maybe she'd make him sit out recess for the rest of his life. That was a scary thought!

He stood outside the principal's office. Maybe she changed into a monster when bad kids came to see her!

Brad made a fist to knock on the door. His hand was shaking.

There was a sudden noise—*ribbit! ribbit!*

Brad jumped. He'd forgotten about the frog in his backpack! He opened the pack. "Quiet!" he whispered. "We're going to see the principal." Then he took a deep breath and knocked on the door.

"Come in," said Dr. Simms.

Slowly, Brad opened the door. "Hi," he said in a small voice. "I'm Brad Farmer."

"Hello, Bradley," said Dr. Simms. "Come on in. Do you know why I called you here?"

Brad put his backpack on a chair. He shook his head. There were too many reasons to choose from.

"I'll give you a hint," said Dr. Simms. "Your mother was here this morning."

Brad's eyes opened wide. His mother? He must be in very big trouble!

Brad opened his mouth, and words just seemed to pour out.

"I'm really sorry about all the bad things I've done," he said. "I'll never put a snake in Eve's lunch box again—or trick Matt, or fool kids with fake signs. Honest!" He crossed his heart.

Dr. Simms looked surprised. "Well, Bradley," she said. "I'm glad you told me all those things. But I called you here because you left this at home."

She picked up a lunch box that was sitting on her desk. "Your mother brought it in for you."

"Oh," Brad said weakly. "Thank you."

"You may go back to your class now," said Dr. Simms. "We can have a nice long talk later."

Brad gulped. He took the lunch box and hurried toward the door.

"Wait!" cried the principal.

Brad froze.

"You forgot your backpack," she said.

Brad let out his breath. "Thanks, Dr. Simms," he said.

"You're welcome," she said, smiling.

Brad smiled back. The principal was nice—not a monster at all. "I really won't do anything bad, ever again," he said. "I promise."

"I'm glad to hear that, Bradley," said Dr. Simms. "I believe you." She picked up the backpack and handed it to him.

"*Ribbit!*" said the backpack.

Reading with Your Child

Even though your child is reading more independently now, it is vital that you continue to take part in this important learning experience.

- Try to read with your child at least twenty minutes each day, as part of your regular routine.
- Encourage your child to keep favorite books in one convenient, cozy spot, so you don't waste valuable reading time looking for them.
- Read and familiarize yourself with the Phonic Guidelines on the next pages.
- Praise your young reader. Be the cheerleader, not the teacher. Your enthusiasm and encouragement are key ingredients in your child's success.

What to Do if Your Child Gets Stuck on a Word

- Wait a moment to see if he or she works it out alone.
- Help him or her decode the word phonetically. Say, "Try to sound it out."
- Encourage him or her to use picture clues. Say, "What does the picture show?"
- Encourage him or her to use context clues. Say, "What would make sense?"
- Ask him or her to try again. Say, "Read the sentence again and start the tricky word. Get your mouth ready to say it."
- If your child still doesn't "get" the word, tell him or her what it is. Don't wait for frustration to build.

What to Do if Your Child Makes a Mistake

- If the mistake makes sense, ignore it—unless it is part of a pattern of errors you wish to correct.
- If the mistake doesn't make sense, wait a moment to see if your child corrects it.
- If your child doesn't correct the mistake, ask him or her to try again, either by decoding the word or by using context or picture clues. Say, "Get your mouth ready" or "Make it sound right" or "Make it make sense."
- If your child still doesn't "get" the word, tell him or her what it is. Don't wait for frustration to build.

Phonic Guidelines

Use the following guidelines to help your child read the words in this story.

Short Vowels

When two consonants surround a vowel, the sound of the vowel is usually short. This means you pronounce *a* as in apple, *e* as in egg, *i* as in igloo, *o* as in octopus, and *u* as in umbrella. Words with short vowels include: *bed, big, box, cat, cup, dad, dog, get, hid, hop, hum, jam, kid, mad, met, mom, pen, ran, sad, sit, sun, top.*

R-Controlled Vowels

When a vowel is followed by the letter *r*, its sound is changed by the *r*. Words with *r*-controlled vowels include: *card, curl, dirt, farm, girl, herd, horn, jerk, torn, turn.*

Long Vowel and Silent E

If a word has a vowel followed by a consonant and an *e*, usually the vowel is long and the *e* is silent. Long vowels are pronounced the same way as their alphabet names. Words with a long vowel and silent *e* include: *bake, cute, dive, game, home, kite, mule, page, pole, ride, vote.*

Double Vowels

When two vowels are side by side, usually the first vowel is long and the second vowel is silent. Words with double vowels include: *boat, clean, gray, loaf, meet, neat, paint, pie, play, rain, sleep, tried.*

Diphthongs

Sometimes when two vowels (or a vowel and a consonant) are side by side, they combine to make a diphthong—a sound that is different from long or short vowel sounds. Diphthongs are: *au/aw, ew, oi/oy, ou/ow*. Words with diphthongs include: *auto, brown, claw, flew, found, join, toy.*

Double Consonants

When two identical consonants appear side by side, one of them is silent. Words with double consonants include: *bell, fuss, mess, mitt, puff, tall, yell.*

Consonant Blends

When two or more different consonants are side by side, they usually blend to make a combined sound. Words with consonant blends include: *bent, blob, bride, club, crib, drop, flip, frog, gift, glare, grip, help, jump, mask, most, pink, plane, ring, send, skate, sled, spin, steep, swim, trap, twin.*

Consonant Digraphs

Sometimes when two different consonants are side by side, they make a digraph that represents a single new sound. Consonant digraphs are: *ch, sh, th, wh*. Words with digraphs include: *bath, chest, lunch, sheet, think, whip, wish*.

Silent Consonants

Sometimes, when two different consonants are side by side, one of them is silent. Words with silent consonants include: *back, dumb, knit, knot, lamb, sock, walk, wrap, wreck*.

Sight Words

Sight words are those words that a reader must learn to recognize immediately—by sight—instead of by sounding them out. They occur with high frequency in easy texts. Sight words include: *a, am, an, and, as, at, be, big, but, can, come, do, for, get, give, have, he, her, his, I, in, is, it, just, like, look, make, my, new, no, not, now, old, one, out, play, put, red, run, said, see, she, so, some, soon, that, the, then, there, they, to, too, two, under, up, us, very, want, was, we, went, what, when, where, with, you*.

Exceptions to the "Rules"

Although much of the English language is phonically regular, there are many words that don't follow the above guidelines. For example, a particular combination of letters can represent more than one sound. Double *oo* can represent a long *oo* sound, as in words such as *boot, cool,* and *moon*; or it can represent a short *oo* sound, as in words such as *foot, good,* and *hook*. The letters *ow* can represent a diphthong, as in words such as *brow, fowl,* and *town*; or they can represent a long *o* sound, as in words such as *blow, snow,* and *tow*. Additionally, some high-frequency words such as *some, come, have,* and *said* do not follow the guidelines at all, and *ough* appears in such different-sounding words as *although, enough,* and *thought*.

The phonic guidelines provided in this book are just that—guidelines. They do not cover all the irregularities in our rich and varied language, but are intended to correspond roughly to the phonic lessons taught in the first and second grades. Phonics provides the foundation for learning to read. Repetition, visual clues, context, and sheer experience provide the rest.